OLIVER AND THE SEA MONKEYS

FOR BIG ADVENTURE AND EVEN BIGGER LAUGHS, READ ALL THE NOT-SO-IMPOSSIBLE TALES

Oliver and the Sea Monkeys

Cakes in Space

Pugs of the Frozen North

A NOT-SO- Impossible Tale!

OLIVER AND THE SEA MONKEYS

BY PHILIP REEVE AND SARAH McINTYRE

A Yearling Book

This is a work of fiction. Names, characters, places, and incidents either are the product of the author's imagination or are used fictitiously. Any resemblance to actual persons, living or dead, events, or locales is entirely coincidental.

Text copyright © 2013 by Philip Reeve
Cover art and interior illustrations copyright © 2013 by Sarah McIntyre

All rights reserved. Published in the United States by Yearling, an imprint of Random House Children's Books, a division of Penguin Random House LLC, New York. Originally published in hardcover as *Oliver and the Seawigs* by Oxford University Press, Oxford, in 2013, and subsequently published in hardcover in the United States by Random House Children's Books, New York, in 2014.

Yearling and the jumping horse design are registered trademarks of Penguin Random House LLC.

Visit us on the Web!
randomhousekids.com

Educators and librarians, for a variety of teaching tools, visit us at
RHTeachersLibrarians.com

The Library of Congress has cataloged the hardcover edition of this work as follows:
Reeve, Philip.
Oliver and the seawigs / by Philip Reeve and Sarah McIntyre. — First Random House edition.
p. cm.
"Originally published in hardcover by Oxford University Press, in 2013."
Summary: "When Oliver's explorer parents go missing, he sets sail on the rescue mission with some new, unexpected friends"—Provided by publisher.
ISBN 978-0-385-38788-0 (trade) — ISBN 978-0-385-38791-0 (lib. bdg.) —
ISBN 978-0-385-38790-3 (ebook)
[1. Adventure and adventurers—Fiction. 2. Islands—Fiction.
3. Mermaids—Fiction. 4. Explorers—Fiction. 5. Missing persons—Fiction.
6. Humorous stories.]
I. McIntyre, Sarah, illustrator. II. Title.
PZ7.R25576Oli 2014 [Fic]—dc23 2013043653

ISBN 978-0-385-38789-7 (pbk.)

Printed in the United States of America

10 9 8 7 6 5 4 3 2 1

First Yearling Edition 2016
This book has been officially leveled by using the F&P Text Level Gradient™ Leveling System.

Random House Children's Books supports the First Amendment
and celebrates the right to read.

FOR ROSE & KI

(AS I PROMISED AT YOUR WEDDING:
CONGRATULATIONS, YOU TWO!)

—SARAH

FOR MARIANNE & HOWARD

—PHILIP

⋆ IF ⋆

THIS ADVENTURE
IS UNDERTAKEN

FAR TOO LIGHTLY,

THE READER HEREBY DISMISSES
THE AUTHORS FROM ALL RESPONSIBILITY
FOR UNTIMELY DEATH OR INJURY
DUE TO DROWNING, KIDNAPPING BY
SEA MONKEYS, OR GENERAL
UNEXPECTED DISAPPEARANCES.

The Management

ONE

Oliver Crisp was only ten years old, but they had been a busy and exciting ten years, because Oliver's mother and father were explorers.

They had met on the top of
Mount Everest.

They had been married
at the Lost Temple of
Amon Hotep, and had spent
their honeymoon searching for the
elephants' graveyard. And when young
Oliver was born, they simply bought themselves a back carrier and an off-road baby
carriage and went right on exploring.

2

But at last there came a day when Mr. and Mrs. Crisp realized there was just nothing left to explore. They had trekked to the headwaters of all the great rivers, and stood on the summits of all the unconquered mountains. Thanks to them, the Lost City of Propacopaketl was lost no longer; the Mystery of the Mokele Mbembe Marshes had been solved. There were no more blank spaces left on the map.

So they packed their belongings aboard their explorermobile and drove home to the house that they owned but had hardly ever lived in, by Deepwater Bay, near the little seaside town of

St. Porrocks. "No more exploring for us," they told each other sadly. "It's time we settled down."

Oliver wasn't sad, though. He was excited. He was tired of living the explorer's life. The house he was coming home to was one he'd only seen on vacations, brief two-week breaks before fresh expeditions. Ten years on the move! No time to make friends, or feel at home anywhere. No time to go to school. He'd never even had a proper bedroom of his own, just a bunk in the back of the explorermobile, and all his things were hidden away in trunks and storage boxes in the spaces under the explorermobile's seats. He thought it would be exciting to have a whole house to live in, and wake up every day to the same view. At Deepwater Bay he would have his own bedroom and bathroom, and he would be starting next term at the school in St. Porrocks. (That might not sound so good to you, but Oliver had never been to school, and he was excited about that too.)

He perched between his parents as Mom steered the explorermobile carefully along the winding lanes. He was waiting for the moment when Deepwater Bay came in sight.

"It's not a very pretty house," his mother reminded him. "It's really rather old and creaky, and the wind blows right through it. It needs lots of work, but we never found the time. Or the money. There's not a lot of money in exploring."

"OK," said Oliver, but he didn't stop feeling excited.

They came over a sudden headland and there it was, the blue bay all dotted with shaggy, steep-sided islands. The house stood at the top of the beach. It was big and gray, with orange lichen dappling its roof.

"Wow!" said Oliver.

"Wow!" said his dad.

"Wow!" said his mom, stopping the explorermobile on a curve of the steep lane and just sitting there, staring in sheer amazement.

"Wow!" they all three said again. Oliver was pleased that his parents sounded just as thrilled as he was. Then he looked at them, and saw that it was not the house that they were looking at, but all those scruffy islands in the bay.

"Where have *they* come from?" asked his father. "I don't remember *them*. . . ."

Mom was rustling the map. "They are not marked here!" she gasped.

"Nine . . . ten . . . fifteen . . . ," Dad muttered. "They must be new islands! Volcanic, probably. . . ."

"Unmapped!" said Mom.

"Uncharted!" said Dad.

"Unexplored!" they whispered, both together.

Oliver sighed. He'd seen them like this before, whenever they heard of a vanished city or a forbidden tomb. Still, he thought, at least they can explore these islands from home. He looked happily at the house while Mom, with her eyes on the islands, started the explorermobile again and took it screeching down the zigzag lane to the beach.

Oliver started unpacking at once. While his mother and father fetched down their inflatable dinghy from the explorermobile's roof, he unlocked the house and carried boxes and bags and suitcases inside. He walked through the big, echoey, dimly familiar rooms, whisking dust sheets off the armchairs that had waited so long for someone to come and sit in them again. He ran upstairs to his room and bounced on the bed. He loved his room already, the way the sunlight came into it and made long golden stripes down the wallpaper. He opened the window to let in the air, and the sea wind, and the cries of the gulls.

"Oliver!" called his mother and

father. They were down at the sea's edge, ready to go off and explore the new islands. They stood in the shallows, waving.

Their inflatable dinghy tossed between them as the waves broke under it. "Oliver! Come with us!"

"I'm busy!" Oliver shouted back. "Why don't you go and have a look around without me? I'll be all right."

He sighed. He knew his parents loved him. It was just that, sometimes, he had the feeling that they loved exploring more.

The little dinghy's outboard motor drowned out the seagulls with its angry-bee buzz as Mom steered through the surf. It circled a small island just offshore, then took off with a roar across the bay towards the larger ones.

Oliver brought his suitcase upstairs and opened it. Carefully he set out his favorite things on shelves and on the windowsill. He arranged his books on the shelf beside his bed. He hung up his clothes in the cupboard. The bars of sunlight moved along the wall. And suddenly Oliver realized that it was quite a long time since he'd heard the outboard or his parents' voices.

He went to the window and leaned out. Deepwater Bay was deserted, and the evening sun shone golden on the waves. There was no sign of Mom and Dad. The islands had vanished. There was only the orange inflatable dinghy, washing back to shore upon the evening tide.

TWO

Most people would be a bit alarmed to find that their parents had disappeared along with a whole bunch of uncharted islands. They might feel inclined to call the police, or the coast guard, or just run about shouting. Not Oliver. He was a Crisp, and made of sterner stuff than that. He hadn't panicked when his baby carriage was carried off by an eagle on the expedition to the Forgotten Mesa. He hadn't lost his cool when his parents took him on that ill-advised cycling trip around the crater of Mount Firebelly. ("But it's supposed to be an *extinct* volcano!" Dad had yelled while lava bombs bounced off their cycling helmets.) He had barely batted an eyelid when a bear stole his sleeping bag on the north face of Mount Rainier. He barely batted one now: just ran downstairs and out onto the beach, looking around in case his parents had come ashore without him noticing.

But the beach, in the wintry afternoon sun, was long and empty and completely parent-free. The orange dinghy rasped against the sand, down on the shore where the small waves kept spreading neat doilies of foam under it.

Oliver pulled it further up the beach and wondered what to do. Then he noticed that there was still one island left in the bay. It was the littlest and lowest and least interesting of them, the one his mom and dad had ignored when they went motoring off to explore the taller ones. Even from the shore, with the low sun shining in his eyes, Oliver could see that they were not on it. But perhaps it held some clue to where they'd gone. . . .

He ran back to the explorermobile and packed a rucksack with Useful Things. Then he locked the house up and put a note on the front door that read:

How he hoped he would be!

He scampered to where the dinghy waited, and shoved it out into the sea again. *Wap, wap* went the waves, slapping its blunt orange nose. Oliver heaved himself aboard. He couldn't work the outboard motor because his arms weren't strong enough to tug the starter cord, but there were oars stowed neatly on the bottom boards and he pulled them out and started rowing. It didn't take him long to reach the island, where he pulled the dinghy up on the sheltered, shoreward side.

The island was just as small as it had looked from the beach. Clumps of grayish grass sighed softly as the sea wind stirred them. There were snaggles of driftwood, festoons of weed, a length of old tarred rope. There was a ramshackle heap of twigs balanced on the pile of boulders that were the highest place on the island. That was all.

It took Oliver less than a minute to walk right across the island to the far shore, where he stood looking out to sea. All his hopes of finding clues faded, like the foam that kept washing around his toes and melting into the wet sand.

"Mom!" he shouted. "Dad!"

The echoes came back at him from the cliffs around the bay. Echoes, but no reply.

"Mom!" he shouted, louder still. "Dad!"

"Oh, put a sock in it, won't you?" grumbled a creaky voice behind him. "Some of us are trying to sleep!"

A pair of beady blue eyes was glaring at Oliver over the brim of that twig heap on the island's crown. The heap was a nest, and the eyes belonged to the bird who owned it.

"But birds don't talk!" protested Oliver.

"Parrots do," the bird said.

"Not really, not properly," Oliver protested. "And anyway, you're not a parrot."

"Indeed I'm not," the bird sniffed.

It stood up in its nest and spread its enormous dirty-white wings. "I am a Wandering Albatross. *Diomedea exulans.* Though you may call me Mr. Culpeper. And now you had best get back to shore, or you will be a wanderer too."

"What does that mean?" Oliver asked.

"Tsk," the bird said, "don't they teach you youngsters anything these days? Not all islands stay where you put them. Some move about. Here one minute, gone the next. This is one of them. That's why I nested on it, of course. I'm not stupid. Why go flapping about the world when I can just roost here and let the island do the wandering?"

Oliver looked down at the island. Between his feet he saw rock, sand, grit, dune grass, and ground-down seashells. It didn't look as if it were going anywhere.

"How do they move?" he asked.

"Who cares?" said Mr. Culpeper, shrugging his wings.

"Where are they going?"

"Who knows?" said Mr. Culpeper. "But all the others have gone already, so this one won't stay much longer."

As he spoke, the island shuddered. Small

stones spilled and rattled, trickling down.

"Hop in your boat and be off with you," said the albatross.

"No!" said Oliver. "Not me. I'm staying. Wherever those islands went, I must go too. My mom and dad were on one of them, you see."

"That noisy couple?" said Mr. Culpeper. "Suit yourself, but you'd be better off without them, if you want *my* opinion."

Oliver wasn't listening anymore. The island lurched, almost throwing him off his feet. He crouched down. He curled his fingers and toes into the sand like roots, clinging on. The island sank a little. Water bubbled whitely around its edges. Then it turned slowly around and started to move out of Deepwater Bay, following the golden pathway that the evening sun had painted on the waves.

As soon as he was used to the movement,

Oliver ran around to where he'd left his boat and made sure it was still safe above the tide line. Looking back, he watched the shore fall swiftly behind. A fiery shard of the sunset reflected for a moment from the window of his own bedroom, and he felt very sad that he would not be sleeping there that night. He almost launched the boat and rowed back to the beach. It was not too far, not quite, not yet. . . . But there would be no point in going home without Mom and Dad. Without them, it wasn't really home at all.

So he turned his back on it, and watched

the sun dip down into the western
sea, and ate a sandwich.

"What's that you're eating?" asked Mr.
Culpeper.

"Tuna mayonnaise," said Oliver.

The albatross snorted. "Newfangled muck."
He spread his wings and soared out over the
ocean in the twilight, dipping down to snatch
a fish out of the waves.

Oliver sat watching the empty sea, hoping
for a glimpse of the other islands. He watched
until it grew too dark to see anything at all,
and then curled up in a grassy space among

the rocks, put his rucksack under his head for a pillow, and slept.

All through the night the island kept moving. Oliver slept soundly, soothed by the island's steady motion and the snore of the sea upon its shores. Then, through his dreams, he heard another sound.

"Doof," it went. And, "Ow!"

Oliver sprang awake. The sky was palest gray, and a few last stars were fading. A wind from the west whispered the grasses.

"Bother!" said someone nearby.

It wasn't Mr. Culpeper. The albatross was sleeping still, safe in his scruffy nest with his head stuffed under his wing.

"Mom?" said Oliver hopefully. "Dad?"

He clambered over the rocks to the beach. There on the shore sat a mermaid, rubbing her nose. "Who put this island here?" she asked.

"Not me," said Oliver.

He had never seen a mermaid before. In

fact he had thought they were just in stories. But then he'd never seen a moving island or a talking *Diomedea exulans* until yesterday, so he wasn't as surprised as he might have been. The mermaid seemed to be about his own age, and she was starting to get a black eye.

"There I was, swimming along, minding my own business," she said, "and suddenly there's an island in the way. It's a danger to shipping, that's what it is. It's a wonder I wasn't knocked unconscious."

"Have you seen any other islands?" asked Oliver. "My mom and dad are on one. I'm looking for them."

"Sorry," said the mermaid. "I didn't even see

this one. My eyesight isn't very good. I can hardly see you. Come over here; you're just a blur."

Oliver went closer. The mermaid frowned at him with vague blue eyes.

"Well," she said, "you're an odd-looking character."

Oliver thought that seemed pretty rich, coming from someone who was at least half fish, but he was a polite boy and did not try to argue. Instead he said, "My name's Oliver."

"Mine's Iris," said the mermaid. "You don't know of a place called Farsight Cove, do you? I was told there's a beach optician there. That's where I was going when your silly island got in my way."

This was not the first time her nearsightedness had got Iris into trouble. Apart from anything else, it made other mermaids laugh at her. Well, it was *one* of the things that made them laugh. All her sisters and cousins were beautiful creatures with eyesight as clear as their singing voices, and they liked to sit on rocks with comb in one hand and mirror in the other and sing eerie songs at passing sailors. Perhaps it was because mer*men* were all rather dull, stay-at-home sorts who didn't much like mermaids' company and preferred to lounge about in their grottoes reading newspapers and discussing the latest finball results. At any rate, the mermaids enjoyed the thought of all those sailors going home and telling everyone about the lovely mermaids who had sung to them, and being haunted by their singing ever after.

Iris was nothing like that at all. She was rather plump, and she could never remember where she'd put her comb and mirror. She couldn't see the point of sitting on rocks and caterwauling all day. The one time she tried singing to a handsome fisherman in his boat, it had turned out not to be a handsome fisherman or a boat at all, just a passing walrus.

"Sorry," she told it. "From a distance you looked just like a little brown boat with a man sitting in it."

"Hmmm," said the walrus. "You need to get your eyes tested, dear." And it told her about the beach optician at Farsight Cove.

Oliver had heard about this beach optician

too. He remembered his mom and dad talking about the dotty old man who wheeled his barrow of eye charts, instruments, and glasses down the path to the cove each day and sat there on the sand, waiting for mermaids. They had laughed and shaken their heads because they didn't believe in mermaids. Oliver looked hard at Iris and decided that there was no way he couldn't believe in her.

"Farsight Cove is quite close to Deep-water Bay ... ," he told her. "But they must both be miles and miles away by now. This island is moving, you see. It's been moving all night."

"Of course it has," said Iris. "It's one of the Rambling Isles."

"The *whats*?"

"The Rambling Isles. They're not really islands at all. They're alive, although they're made of stone. They wander the oceans, and they're always getting mistaken for ordinary islands, but really they're more like very big stony giants."

"Oh," said Oliver. "Well, where is it going?"

"How on earth should I know?" asked Iris. "You really do say the strangest things. I expect it's just rambling around, collect-ing stuff. That's what Rambling Isles *do*.

But I suppose you could always ask it."

Oliver looked around, bewildered.

How could he ask rocks and stones and grass where they were going? Well, he could ask them, but how could he expect them to reply?

"Oh, I'll do it," said Iris wearily. She slapped the nearest rock as hard as she could. "Hello?" she shouted.

The movement of the island changed. It slowed and turned from side to side. Mr. Culpeper woke up with a squawk and demanded to know what was happening.

Slowly the island lifted from the sea. There was a rush and gurgle of falling water draining from its edges. It rose cliff-high and the waves rolled past it far below. Oliver went to its raggedy edge and looked over.

He saw that the island was really just the top of a vast, stony head. The grass was its hair.

Water ran down its face; limpets stubbled
its cheeks; seaweed and old carrier bags were
tangled in its bushy eyebrows. Two big eyes
peered up at Oliver.

THREE

Oliver was startled (and Oliver was *not* a boy who startled easily). "It's got a face!"

"Of course it's got a face," said Iris.

Oliver waved at the Rambling Isle. "Um . . . ," he said.

"Hello," Iris told it. "He wants to know where you're going."

The Rambling Isle watched them thoughtfully. It wasn't used to being talked to. It was years and years since it had spoken. It hadn't even realized

37

that there was anybody on its head until these two small upside-down faces appeared.

"Please," said Oliver, "I have to find those other islands. My mom and dad were on one. That's why I need to know where you're all going."

The Rambling Isle opened its cave of a mouth. It cleared its throat with a crumbly rumble like masses of rock shearing and shifting deep in the earth. "*They* are all going to the Hallowed Shallows," it said, "for the Night of the Seawigs."

Oliver was starting to feel dizzy, hanging upside down like that. He sat upright. "What's a seawig?" he asked.

"Haven't you heard?" said Iris. "Every seven years the Rambling Isles all gather together at the Hallowed Shallows to show off their treasures. They love to collect things, you see; all the bits of flotsam that the sea washes up on their heads. They're very proud of their collections. On the Night of the Sea-wigs, each of them wears a wig made of all the treasures it has gathered on its travels. The one with the finest wig is declared the winner. It is a great honor. Everyone makes a huge fuss over them. They become Chief Island for the next seven years, and they get to order the other islands about if they want to and choose all the best bits of wig for themselves."

"I bet Thrumcap wins this time," said the island. "Or Dimsey. They always have the best seawigs. Of course, *they* have crinkly, complicated coastlines. All sorts of interesting things get stuck on *them*. Most of what washes up on my shores washes straight off again. Look at me! All I have to show for my wanderings are a few bits of old rope and a stupid bird's nest."

Oliver tried to think of something encouraging he could say that would cheer up the poor island, but it was true: its wig was a mess. Its summit was mostly bald rock, with those tussocks of grassy hair sprouting here and there, and rather a lot of albatross poo, now that Oliver came to look critically at it.

"Who are you talking to?" asked Mr. Culpeper, stalking importantly down the beach. "And whose nest is he calling stupid?"

"I don't even know whether I can be bothered making the journey," the island went on in its deep and mournful voice. "You can't imagine the wonderful seawigs that will be on display at the Hallowed Shallows. And there I'll be, with my bit of rope and my bird's nest. The others will all laugh at me. Perhaps I'll just give it a miss this time."

"No!" said Oliver. He hung over the beach edge again. "You must go! Or at least tell me how to get there, so I can find Mom and Dad!"

"Oh, it's not a place you could get to," said Iris airily. "Not on your own." She hung upside down beside him with her wet hair dangling. "The Hallowed Shallows aren't that sort of place at all. They are the place where all the old things of the sea went to live once people in your world stopped believing in them. Actually they are where I live too, only I came out to find that optician, and I couldn't, and now I can't find my way home either." She blinked nearsightedly. Oliver thought he saw tears beginning to gather in her eyes.

41

He fetched the oily length of nylon rope he'd noticed on the tide line yesterday. He tied one end firmly around a rock, then lowered himself down in front of the island's face.

"Did you hear that?" he said. "We both need to go to the Hallowed Shallows. Please say you'll take us there."

"Oh, I don't know ... ," said the island glumly.

Oliver frowned, swaying in front of those huge eyes like a hypnotist's watch. "Look, do you have a name?" he asked.

"Me?" said the island dolefully. "A name? No. Some of the bigger Rambling Isles have been mistaken for real islands by sailors and explorers, who gave them the most splendid names, but no one ever noticed me."

"Not at all?" said Iris.

"Well, someone put a sign up on me once, when I went to sleep for a few years near the mouth of a river.

"But it fell off. Anyway, I can't go around calling myself 'Danger: Submerged Rocks,' can I?"

"Well, you need a name," said Oliver, looking up at those craggy features, at the clinging barnacles and clumps of weed. "I'm going to call you . . . Cliff."

"Cliff . . . ," said the island, trying it out. He sounded pleased. *"Cliff . . ."*

"Now listen, Cliff," said Oliver. "How long is it till this Seawigs contest?"

"We gather at the Shallows tomorrow night," said Cliff.

Iris nodded. "That's right. All my mermaid friends are going. They're going to perch on rocks and sing; it's completely lame."

"Well then, Cliff," said Oliver, "you've got all of today and tomorrow to gather some really brilliant things to decorate your seawig. We'll help!"

"Will you?" sniffed the poor island, looking hopefully at him.

"Will we?" asked Iris.

"Course we will," said Oliver. "Let's think. What would be the best things you could possibly have on your wig? You've already got me, and Iris, and the inflatable dinghy. . . ."

"He's got an albatross too," said Iris. "It

can stand on the top and spread its wings or something."

"Excuse me," said Mr. Culpeper, coming to peer over the edge beside her. "I am *Diomedea exulans*, I am, and a particularly fine specimen too. I am not some funfair attraction! 'Spread its wings,' indeed." He sniffed loudly. "It seems to me that this island has gone to the dogs. It used to be such a nice, quiet place. Now I can hardly move for boys and mermaids. I don't like the sound of this Seawigs affair at all. It sounds like a lot of noise and bother to me."

"Don't listen to him," Oliver told the island. "Just think! What are the most wonderful things that an island could wear?"

"Well, there's always shipwrecks," said Cliff. "Shipwrecks are very stylish."

"The dinghy is a sort of wreck," Oliver pointed out.

"It's just stranded," said Cliff sadly. "That's not the same thing at all."

"He's right," said Iris dreamily, draping her tail in a rock pool. "What he needs is a really spectacular wreck. What about the *Water Mole*?"

Oliver frowned. "I've heard of that. It was the world's first submarine. The king of Spain built it to ferry treasure from his gold mines without English pirates noticing, but it didn't work too well. It sank, and nobody knows where." Iris coughed and pointed modestly to herself.

"You mean, you know where we could find it?" Oliver asked.

"I ran into it while I was swimming

around," Iris said, rubbing thoughtfully at a fading bruise upon her elbow. "It's on an undersea mountain not far from here."

"Ooh, a submarine?" said Cliff, sounding hopeful for the first time. "I don't think any of the other islands has a submarine!"

"Well, let's go and find the *Water Mole*," said Oliver, "and then hurry to the Hallowed Shallows and see what those other isles think of it! I bet they'll declare you the winner in an instant!"

Cliff nodded happily, almost tumbling his two passengers off into the sea. He'd never really thought of himself as a winner of anything before, but Oliver spoke with such certainty that he could almost hear the voices of his fellow Rambling Isles as they cheered his wonderful wig. He sank back down into the waves until the top of his stony head became an island once again, and with Iris shouting directions, he set off, surging through the water with a steady, confident motion.

Oliver lay on the edge of the beach and looked down through the water. He could dimly see Cliff's huge, rocky limbs moving far beneath him in the depths. How strange to think there were such things as Rambling Isles in the world, and he had never even heard of them!

FOUR

After Cliff had been striding along for an hour or two, Oliver saw a shape on the sea ahead. Then another. They looked like small, stony islands, but he couldn't be certain of that anymore. He pointed the islands out to Iris. "Are they more Rambling Isles?"

The mermaid peered in the direction he was pointing. "I think they were once," she said. "But they've settled down."

"What does that mean?"

"It means just what it sounds like. Some of

them lose the urge to keep wandering. They give up collecting bits and pieces for their sea-wigs. And once they stop moving, they sort of take root; silt and sand pile up around their feet, and weed grows on them, and coral, and there they stay."

One of the settled islands was quite close now. Looking down through the waves, Oliver thought he could see its stony face, blurred by weed and masked with barnacles.

"Are they dead?" he asked. "Or just asleep?"

"They're settled," said Iris. "They are just islands now."

"I hope Cliff never settles," said Oliver. "I like him rambling about. I wouldn't want him to be just an island."

"Oh, don't worry," Iris said, and swished her tail in the rock pool, cleaning the sand from between her scales. "Once he has the

Water Mole on top of him, he'll win for sure. It's completely brilliant."

Oliver nodded, hoping she was right. Then a bad thought struck him. "Iris? How can you find your way back to this submarine wreck if you can't even find your own way home?"

"I can smell it, silly," said Iris. "It's in a very smelly patch of sea. Can't *you* smell it yet?"

Oliver sniffed. Sure enough there was a scent on the air of green things growing and rotting.

Hour after hour the scent grew stronger, and that afternoon they saw a darkness that lay like a green shadow on the sea ahead. Soon it stretched from horizon to horizon. As they entered its outer fringes, Oliver realized that the whole face of the ocean was clogged with drifting weed.

"We must be in the Sargasso Sea!" he said

excitedly. "Sailors fear it because their ships get becalmed here, and the weed tangles around them and traps them."

"No, this is a completely different place," said Iris. "It's called the Sarcastic Sea, and sailors fear it because the weed keeps making horrid, hurtful comments about them."

Sure enough, as Cliff carried them deeper into the weed, they began to hear its little mocking voices calling out to them.

"Oh, a *mermaid*! That's *just* what we need!" and "Nice seawig, mate!" and "I love the inflatable dinghy. Orange is such a *tasteful* color." And you could tell that it didn't mean any of the things it said—in fact it meant exactly the opposite, and all its comments were followed by scornful snickers, or whispery conversations that ended in laughter. The weed of the Sarcastic Sea was very sarcastic weed indeed.

As Cliff plowed onwards, great clumps of

the stuff began piling up on the beach, and Oliver noticed that as well as the little bladders that helped to keep ordinary types of seaweed afloat, its strands were dotted with beady eyes, which all looked witheringly at him. He took out his notebook and made a sketch, knowing that his mom and dad would be interested when he found them.

But the weeds did not much like being snagged on Cliff's beaches, because once they were out of the waves, Mr. Culpeper stalked around pecking at the tiny crabs and water bugs that lived among them.

Hey!

they squeaked.

Watch it with the beak!

Ow!

Oliver felt sorry for the weed, and he and Iris began making their way around Cliff's shores, shoveling it back into the waves and getting precious little thanks.

The floating weed soon learned to keep out of the way of the oncoming island. It drew back to make a path for Cliff, and by the time Iris told him to stop, there was a broad patch of clear water all around him.

"This is the place," the mermaid said.

"Are you sure?" asked Oliver. This bit of the Sarcastic Sea looked just the same as all the rest to him.

"Two currents meet here," replied Iris primly. "The sea smells different. The *Water Mole* is right beneath us. Come and see for yourself, if you don't believe me."

So Oliver fetched his swimming things and goggles, took a deep breath, and plunged after Iris into the waves, where a few small, left-behind strands of seaweed still floated, sneering, "Those swim trunks really suit you (I *don't* think). . . ."

With a flick of her tail Iris went racing down into the green shadows. She was a clumsy thing on dry land, but in the water she was lithe and nimble.

Oliver struggled after her, down past Cliff's huge, watchful face, until, far below, he started to make out the summits of drowned mountains rising dimly from the ocean deeps.

By the time he saw them, the breath that Oliver had taken before he dived had almost run out. His eyes bulged and his heart hammered. Bubbles seeped from the corners of his mouth and swam towards the surface like silver jellyfish. Then, in the last instant before he had to follow them, he glimpsed the wreck. The *Water Mole* lay on the rocky top of one of those mountains. Weed and coral had transformed its hull into a strange underwater cathedral. Fish darted in and out of the shattered windows at the stern, and an eel as stripy as a witch's tights had tied itself like a bow around the figurehead.

Iris bumped into the cabin, groped her way up a ladder, and perched on the top, beaming up at Oliver as if to say, "I told you so!" But Oliver could stay no longer in her underwater world. He kicked his legs and shot back to the surface in a rush of bubbles, bursting out into the sunshine and taking deep gulps of fresh, delicious air.

Cliff rose out of the sea beside him, with falls of white water cascading off his brow.

"It's there!" said Oliver, treading water in front of the island's nose. "It's lovely! It will make an *awesome* wig!"

But how were they to lift it? Raising wrecks was difficult, Oliver knew that. He'd seen Cliff's clumsy, stony hands. He was afraid they'd crush the *Water Mole* to splinters if Cliff simply tried to pick it up.

"You must go down to it," he said.

"Go under the sea?" said Cliff, eyes widening. "But what about my sands? My shells? My bits of rope? They'll all wash off if I go under!"

"And more to the point, what about my *nest*?" demanded Mr. Culpeper, circling above Oliver's head.

"I know!" said Oliver. He scrambled back up onto Cliff's beach and quickly gathered anything that looked as if it might float away, including the albatross's nest. He dumped it all into the dinghy and then climbed in with it.

Then, while Iris swam about below directing things (she wasn't much help because her eyesight was even worse underwater than it was above, but she liked to feel important), Cliff knelt down on his gigantic underwater knees and let the waves of the Sarcastic Sea swirl over his head. Oliver put on his goggles again and hung over the edge of his dinghy with his face in the sea as the waters lifted it. Down in the green gloom far below, he saw Cliff carefully edge his way towards the wreck, and glimpsed the flash of Iris's

rainbow tail as she circled, gesturing at Cliff to move left a bit, right a bit, stop, come forwards. . . . (She didn't realize that she had her back to Cliff. She was actually gesturing at a confused-looking whale that just happened to be passing.)

Cliff went right up to the wreck. He nudged it with his head and tugged at it with his stumpy, stony arms. At last it shifted and rolled gently sideways.

Oliver jumped up. "That's it!" he hooted, although Oliver knew the Rambling Isle couldn't hear him. "You've done it! Now come up!"

Cliff settled the weight of the ancient submarine on his head and began to rise, carefully, carefully, with swirls of sand glittering in the sea around him. He came up under the dinghy in a great roaring and rushing and bubbling of water and a flopping and floundering of stranded fish. Most of them were washed back into the sea as Cliff continued to rise and the waters poured off him. Soon there was beach beneath Oliver's dinghy again. On the top of Cliff's head lay the *Water Mole*, all wet and startling and shiny in the sunlight. The striped eel had slithered off and the gilded bowsprit glimmered faintly, pointing at the sky.

It was the finest wig an island ever wore.

"Yay!" shouted Oliver, jumping out of the submarine and doing a victory dance among the rock pools.

"Yay!" said Iris, flopping ashore and wringing out her hair.

"Yay!" rumbled Cliff, and "Yay!" cawed Mr. Culpeper. Only the sarcastic strands of floating weed were unimpressed. "Showy," they complained, still keeping a safe distance from Cliff's shores. "Shipwrecks are *so* last season." But they were only seaweed, so who cared what they thought?

Then Mr. Culpeper, gliding down to perch on the coral-encrusted flagstaff, said suddenly, "What's that?"

Oliver turned to look. There behind him on the weedy sea, an island stood. He could not believe that he hadn't noticed it before.

FiVE

It was not really an island, of course. It was another Rambling Isle, and it had crept out of a nearby fog bank and sneaked up behind Cliff while everyone was distracted by the raising of the submarine.

Although Oliver did not recognize it, it was one of the same islands that had been resting in Deepwater Bay the day his parents disappeared. He had not been able to see it from his bedroom window because the headland hid it, but Mr. and Mrs. Crisp had seen it as they motored away from the beach in their dinghy and had steered straight towards it, because they could tell at once that it was easily the most interesting.

It was tall and rocky, and on its summit dark trees clustered. Among the trees stood a ruined temple, crumbly and overgrown. Around the temple towered huge stone heads with empty eyes and open mouths. They looked a bit like the famous statues on Easter Island. (In fact they were where the Easter Islanders had got the idea from, for this Rambling Isle had passed close to Easter Island long ago.)

"Remarkable!" Oliver's dad had shouted as the dinghy bounced across the waves of Deepwater Bay. "Polynesian? Pre-Columbian?"

"A whole unknown civilization!" declared Oliver's mom, snapping photos of those weird stone heads as the dinghy swept into the island's shadow and they circled it, searching for a place to land.

There was a beach on the seaward side. A beach of black sand, with steps carved in the cliff behind it, winding up past crumbled walls and watchful statues to those strange ruins on the summit.

Poor foolish Crisps! They were so eager to explore that they did not bother dragging their dinghy up above the tide line, which everyone knows is one of the first rules of exploring. They just left it there upon the shining sand and ran up those stairs. The clicking of their cameras echoed among the ruins, and so did their excited cries, until they reached the ruined temple.

It was not quite as ruined as it had looked from sea level. Someone had put double glazing in its windows, and a chimney poked from the roof, puffing out little curlicues of wood smoke.

71

"Oh! This island is inhabited!" said Oliver's dad, trying not to sound too disappointed, even though he had hoped to be the first person to discover a lost civilization.

"But inhabited by whom?" asked his wife, imagining lost tribes, priest-kings, and ancient wisdom.

That was when the island shivered. That was when it shook. "Earthquake!" cried Mrs. Crisp, and "Volcano!" yelled her husband. The island sank a little. Down on its shore, waves swirled up the beach, lifted the abandoned dinghy, and carried it gently out into the bay. And from the open mouths of all those stone heads there came a noise: a rustling, a whispering, a scrabbling, a jostling, a strange, demented jabbering that grew louder and louder as the island started moving out to sea. . . .

And now here it stood, a few hundred yards from Cliff, with Oliver staring at it in surprise.

"Look at all those creepy old heads!" said Iris.

Cliff turned beneath them, looking. "Oh dear!" he rumbled. "Oh no! It's the Thurlstone!"

"What's the Thurlstone?" asked Oliver.

"It is very old, and very bad," Cliff said. "Bad men did human sacrifices in that temple on its top long ago, and the blood trickled down inside it and turned it wicked. They say it's quite hollow, and rotten to the core. Oh dear!"

The Thurlstone lifted itself a little way out of the water. Massive weedy shoulders rose into the sunlight. Water drained out through cracks and fissures in the isle's sides. Its mean black eyes stared hard at Cliff through veils of falling water. A mouth like a sea cave opened and a stony voice said, "Nice shipwreck you have there."

"It's ours!" Iris shouted back. "We found it!"

Her voice sounded very small and thin and shrill after the thunder of the Thurlstone's. It boomed again. "Don't like the mermaid, though," it said. "Mermaids are vulgar."

Now that he came to look properly at it, Oliver saw that the Thurlstone

was wearing quite an elaborate seawig. Loads of plaited seaweed were arranged around its cliffs, glittering with bits of broken glass and shiny metal. Old flip-flops dangled from the branches of those dark and twisted trees, and among the rocks where the temple stood a trawler and a rusty battleship were perched. From the cliffs on either side of its face two big glass globes dangled in cradles of knotted rope, like earrings, or baubles on a Christmas tree. Inside the globes, something moved.

Oliver snatched his rucksack and ferreted inside it for his binoculars. He focused on one of those glassy danglers. The thing inside it was his mom. He yelped and swung the binoculars. There inside the other globe was Dad. The explorers seemed quite unharmed. Oliver began to jump up and down on the beach. He waved and shouted. When he looked through the binoculars again, he saw that his mom had spotted him. He saw his dad scribble something in his explorer's notebook and press it flat against the inside of his glass prison for Oliver to read.

Now his mother was scribbling too, and pressing a note of her own to the glass.

But the Thurlstone was coming closer. Ignoring mean comments and backhanded compliments from the floating weed, it shouldered its way through the sea. Octopuses writhed their tentacles among its eyebrows, and a shark fell out of its nose like a fierce booger. Up on its forehead a little platform had been built, and there a boy stood, looking down.

The Thurlstone was so close by then that Oliver didn't need his binoculars anymore. He could see the boy quite clearly without them. He was older than Oliver: a tall teenager, balancing precariously on bean-sprout legs and about to tumble clumsily into adulthood. He wore sea boots and a sailor's uniform with all sorts of gold braid and medals and fancy finery all over it.

When the gap of open water between Cliff and the Thurlstone had narrowed to a stone's throw, the Thurlstone stopped in a swirl of foam and spoke again. "Want it," it said, staring at the *Water Mole*.

Up on its brow the boy picked up a big brass megaphone and bellowed through it.

MY ISLAND WANTS THAT
WRECK OF YOURS. YOU'D
BETTER HAND IT OVER.

"Ooh, of all the cheek!" squealed Iris. "We found it! It's ours!"

"You're not having my wig!" rumbled Cliff.

Oliver just cupped his hands around his mouth and shouted, "Give me back my mom and dad!"

The other boy threw back his head and laughed. It was the sort of laugh that told you instantly he was not about to let poor Mr. and Mrs. Crisp go. "Ha ha ha!" he cackled. "So they are yours, are they? Well, you should have taken better care of them. They make nice additions to the Thurlstone's seawig, don't you think? But not as nice as that fine submarine your island's found. Hand it over now, and spare yourself a lot of unpleasantness."

79

"Who are you, anyway?" asked Iris. "You're very full of yourself."

"My name," the boy said importantly, "is Stacey de Lacey."

"But that's a girl's name!" blurted Oliver.

Stacey de Lacey's face turned a dark shade of red. "Silence!" he shouted. "Stacey is one of those names that can be for a boy or a girl! Like Hilary, or Leslie, or . . . um . . . Anyway, when the Night of the Seawigs rolls around, my Thurlstone shall have the finest wig of all! That submarine is just the thing we need to top it off, and if you won't give it to us, we shall just have to take it!"

"Mad," said Iris in an undertone, "quite mad."

Stacey de Lacey clapped his hands. "Come, my lovelies!" he shouted, and laughed with wicked glee.

From the giant statues that grinned and snarled upon the Thurlstone's massive head, there came a rustling, a whispering, a scrabbling, a jostling, a strange, demented jabbering. . . .

No wonder Stacey de Lacey sounded gleeful. It was quite a new feeling for him, giving orders. When he'd been growing up, nobody had ever taken much notice of him. His parents, who were rich and busy, barely paid him any attention. The other children at school all hated him. And why did they hate him? Well, actually it was because he was a nasty, boastful bully, but Stacey didn't realize that: he was sure it was just because of his name. "Stacey can be a boy's name too," he would tell them when they laughed at it. They never believed him. Angry and all alone, he took long walks on the beach near his house, dreaming of the terrible revenge he would take on them when he was older.

All sorts of things washed up on that beach. As Stacey de Lacey strode along with his hands in his pockets, he was forever kicking aside old flip-flops, fisherman's floats, and plastic bottles with mysterious foreign labels. One day, after a storm, he found a shingle covered with stinking seaweed, uprooted from some deep hollow of the seabed. It was a type of seaweed that he had never noticed before. It had thick stalks, each as tall as Stacey, with a fat green bulb at the top. Stacey picked up one of the stalks and began cracking it like a bullwhip as he stomped along. He imagined lashing his classmates with it.

"Stacey is *not* a girl's name!" he shouted. *Crack!* "You'll be sorry when I'm famous and powerful!" he yelled. *Crack!* "Just you wait!" he hollered. "One day I'll . . ."

Crack, squelch, splat!

The green bulb at the end of the sea whip burst and out came a splurt of dirty water, and something else, something that *moved*, scrabbling and burrowing its way down into the tangles of dead weed that were heaped along the tide line.

Stacey went closer and prodded the weed piles with his toe. Something was definitely rustling around in there. He bent down for a closer look. Suddenly the weed was torn aside and a hideous little fanged and grinning face stared up at him. Then two little web-fingered hands seized the toe of his sneaker and the creature sank its teeth into the rubber.

"Yow!" shouted Stacey de Lacey, doing a triple backwards somersault in his surprise. The creature flew off his shoe. By the time he had clambered up and dusted the sand out of his eyes, it was crouching on a nearby rock, watching him. It looked like an ugly little monkey with webbed hands and feet and greasy green fur.

"Get lost!" he yelled angrily.

The sea monkey cowered and crept away over the top of the rock, out of sight.

Stacey was impressed. He wasn't used to people doing what he told them.

"Come back!" he shouted.

The monkey reappeared.

"My name is Stacey de Lacey," he said, and watched the monkey suspiciously. It didn't laugh; it didn't even giggle.

"Stacey is not a girl's name!" he said. Still nothing. Feeling encouraged, he told it, "You're mine! You will do everything I say!"

The monkey drew itself to attention and saluted.

If Stacey de Lacey had been a different sort of boy, he might have thought, "I've found a friend!" But Stacey had never really wanted friends. He thought, "I've found a servant!"

He looked around.

All about him, the beach was littered with whips of the strange weed, each with its sea-green bulb. Was there a monkey in every one? There must be loads of them! Hundreds! He picked up a strand and squeezed the bulb until it popped like a pimple.

Out tumbled another monkey. Excit-edly, Stacey popped another, and

then another. "Help me!" he ordered the chittering, jittering monkeys, and they

ran with him along the tide line, squeezing and popping, squeezing and popping, until a

whole army of sea mon-
keys was scut-
tling behind him.

Stacey de Lacey
knew his parents

would never let him keep
anything as stinky and
repulsive-looking as these
monkeys. Luckily, there
was a particularly large
and slimy rock pool that
he knew of, around the

curve of the cliffs, where nobody but him ever went. He led the monkeys there and watched them pour into the pool. They were as happy underwater as above it. They crouched in the shadows of the pool and looked up at Stacey with wicked, wary eyes.

"I am your master!" he said proudly.

After that, Stacey de Lacey turned his thoughts to the sea. If sea monkeys were real, then what other strange things might the oceans hold? Between trips to the rock pool, where he fed and gloated over his growing monkey-band, he talked to sailors at the harbor. He peered at old books in secret libraries. He learned of the Hallowed Shallows. He learned of mermaids and drowned cities. He learned of the Rambling Isles, and of the gathering that they held on the Night of the Seawigs.

"Monkeys are all very well," said Stacey de Lacey to himself, "but if I had my own Rambling Isle, think how powerful I'd be then!" He liked the idea of roving the world on his own island, being mean to people.

So he started scouring the beach for interesting things the sea washed up and leaving them above the tide line on a tall rock just offshore. If the Night of the Seawigs was real, he thought, no Rambling Isle would be able to resist such top-notch wig ingredients. And sure enough, one foggy evening, he heard great sloshing footsteps move through the waves towards that rock, and saw a giant shape moving in the mist. He heard the Rambling Isle grumbling to itself as it sifted through the pile of driftwood and old fishing nets he'd left. "This stuff's no good," he heard it say. "This won't help me win. . . ."

"Hey, Island!" shouted Stacey de Lacey. The grumbling stopped. The thing in the fog stood listening. "You want to win this stupid Seawigs thing?" Stacey yelled. "You should steal the best stuff from other islands' wigs. And if you can't do that, just nobble them: ruin their wigs so they can't win!"

As luck would have it, the island Stacey was talking to was none other than the bad old Thurlstone, meanest of all the Rambling Isles. The Thurlstone liked the way this boy thought. "How?" it asked.

"With my help!" said Stacey, and as the Thurlstone loomed out of the fog to peer down at him, he spread his arms out proudly to show it the gibbering, jabbering swarm of monkeys crowded on the shingle behind him.

"I have an army of monkeys!" he said.

* * *

That's what the green tide was, pouring out of the mouths and eyes of the Thurlstone's old stone heads and rushing across the sea. Sea monkeys! Small and smelly in their coats of greasy green fur, they giggled horribly as they swam towards Cliff, or scampered across the mats of drifting weed. "Don't mind us," grumbled the weed mats, but the sea monkeys were immune to sarcasm.

Up Cliff's beaches they rushed, knocking poor Iris off her rock.

They sank their teeth and claws into the orange inflatable dinghy and popped it, just for laughs. Oliver tried to stop them. He picked up monkeys and hurled them back at the sea, but more were landing all the time and they were scary and dangerous-looking. They bared their dirty yellow fangs and screeched at him.

The monkey tide sloshed up onto Cliff's bouldery summit and lapped around the *Water Mole*. The sea monkeys were so small that Oliver did not think they could shift the submarine, but there were so many of them that they did. The *Water Mole* lifted from its perch, afloat again on a sea of snot-green fur. Oliver and Iris had to jump out of the way as the chattering monkeys rushed back with it into the sea. The Thurlstone dipped down, until only Stacey's balcony and the old stones and the trees around the temple showed, and the monkeys swam and swirled and struggled and shoved the *Water Mole* onto his head.

"So long, losers!" called Stacey de Lacey. "We'll see you at the Hallowed Shallows— if you still think it's worth turning up, of course."

The Thurlstone turned and moved off. The glass orbs that were Oliver's parents' prisons bobbed on either side of it, towed on their tethers of rope, with Mr. and Mrs. Crisp waving sad goodbyes inside them. Sea monkeys went scurrying back to their nests in the old stone heads. The *Water Mole* shone so brightly in the slanting sunlight that Oliver could see the gleam of it long after the wicked island had dwindled to a speck on the horizon.

That went well! said the watching weed.

SIX

As the Thurlstone vanished, all Cliff's newfound hopefulness drained away. The fight went out of him. Iris and Oliver felt him slump. They couldn't blame him. Poor old giant! So much of his golden sand and drifts of flotsam had been washed away when he stooped to fetch the *Water Mole*. Now that it was gone, his stony head was even barer than before.

"Now what shall we do?" asked Iris.

"Go after that Thurlstone, of course!" shouted Oliver. "Quick, Cliff! Follow him!"

Cliff lifted his cave mouth out of the waves to say, "What's the point? He's beaten me." Then he subsided again.

"You can't just let him win!" said Oliver. "Is he the sort of island who deserves to win the Night of the Seawigs? And as for that Stacey de Lacey . . . ! Go after them, and get the *Water Mole* back!"

"How?" rumbled Cliff. "They have an army of monkeys."

"He's got a point," said Iris.

"Then go to the Hallowed Shallows!" insisted Oliver. "Tell everyone what Stacey and his Thurlstone did. . . ."

"They won't listen to me," said Cliff wearily. "They'll be too busy admiring the Thurlstone's marvelous seawig and laughing at me."

"So what are you going to do?" Iris asked.

Cliff sighed. "I'm going to settle," he decided.

"No!" yelled Oliver.

"I should have done it years ago," Cliff went on. "What's the point of all this tramping around, collecting stuff? I'm going to stand here and grow roots and forget I ever was a rambler. I'll become just an island. That's all I'm good for. I'm useless. Finished. Washed up." He sank back slowly into the sea.

"No!" shouted Oliver again. He did a dance of frustration, shin-deep in the wavelets that washed Cliff's shores. But no amount of stamping or shouting would make Cliff come up again. Oliver remembered the sad, lifeless, settled isles that Iris had shown him on the way to the Sarcastic Sea. He imagined the sand and silt slowly piling up around Cliff's feet.

"Oh dear," said Iris, with salt tears

dripping off her chin. "I think he means it."

"*Now* look what you've done," sniffed Mr. Culpeper, fussily rearranging his nest, which had been terribly knocked about by those swarming sea monkeys. "If you hadn't dragged us here in search of that stupid wreck, this would never have happened. It's all your fault."

"Well, I'm not going to let Stacey de Lacey win," said Oliver. Years of exploring had taught him that you don't solve problems by sitting around complaining about them. You have to *do* something. That's how his mom and dad had saved him from that Komodo dragon. That's how they'd escaped from the dungeons of M'bumbi M'bumbi. He struck an explorer-ish pose on the shore and said, "I'm going to go after that Thurlstone and show it that it can't just go around snitching other people's shipwrecks and kidnapping moms and dads!"

"That's all very well and good," said Iris, "but ARMY OF MONKEYS, remember? Oh, and your boat's gone all flop."

Oliver ignored the reminder about the monkeys. He hadn't yet thought of any way that he could deal with them. He had an answer to the part about the boat, though. He opened his explorer's rucksack and triumphantly pulled out a foot pump and a Punctured Dinghy Repair Kit. One hour of patching and pumping later, he was ready. He shoved the dinghy into the waves and hoisted himself aboard. He tugged the motor's starter cord.

It didn't work. It never did. You needed big muscly arms like Dad's to make it start.

Iris looked on doubtfully. "I suppose I could help," she said.

"Oh yes, you'll be a lot of use!" snapped Oliver, so sarcastically that even the seaweed was shocked. "Your arms are even feebler than mine!"

"Oh, I don't mean like that," sniffed the mermaid. She unhooked the motor from the stern of the dinghy and dropped it on the shore. Then, before Oliver could ask how that was supposed to help, she scrambled half aboard the dinghy, with her tail hanging off behind.

"Shove off!" she said.

"Ooh, isn't she *rude!*" whispered the weed admiringly.

"I mean shove the *dinghy* off."

Oliver shoved. As the dinghy drifted into deeper water, Iris started to flap her tail up and down, driving them away from the shore.

It was difficult to steer at first, but they soon worked it out. Iris took the dinghy on a farewell circuit of the island. Oliver looked over the side, down through the waves at the great, dim cliff face of Cliff's face looming there. He couldn't see if Cliff's eyes were open or closed. He couldn't tell if the Rambling Isle was watching his friends leave, or just too sad to care. He waved anyway.

Mr. Culpeper flapped over to perch on the dinghy's prow. "I might as well come with you," he said. "After all, you'll need help finding that thieving island, I suppose."

So the albatross took off again, soaring towards the horizon, and the mermaid-powered dinghy followed him, splashing along the lane of open water that the Thurlstone had left through the sarcastic weed.

It was tiring work for poor Iris. Every few minutes she had to stop and rest while Oliver refueled her by feeding her caramel bars from his lunch box. But at last the Sarcastic Sea was left behind.

"I wonder why Stacey de Lacey is so keen to help the Thurlstone win the contest, anyway?" wondered Oliver. But Iris was too busy being an outboard motor to reply.

Mr. Culpeper flew above them, calling down directions. At first there was no need, for Oliver and Iris could see the Thurlstone far ahead. But as the day wore on, the thieving isle drew away from them, and a strange haze arose. Soon it was hard for even the sharp-eyed albatross to see very far. "We are coming near to the Hallowed Shallows," said Iris.

They began to pass other Rambling Isles. At first they looked like normal islands, but they were all moving, and all in the same direction, with white wakes of foam stretching behind them. Some were as small and tatty as Cliff. Some were magnificent. There was one who had sculpted a sort of volcano on his upper parts, and lit a fire in it so trails of smoke rings mingled with the haze. There was one who had drizzled wet sand onto her head to build up teetering pinnacles and spires, and another who had arranged miles and miles of weed into a massive beehive, with a small ship stuck in the middle of it. None of them paid the slightest attention to the dinghy.

"If only Cliff was here!" said Oliver, feeling sad that they had left their own Rambling Isle behind.

"The rest would only laugh at him," said Iris. "Some of those seawigs are to die for!"

* * *

Meanwhile, back in the Sarcastic Sea, Cliff was thinking sadly of his friends. He had never had actual *people* living on him before, and he missed them now that they were gone. Not only that, the seaweed had drifted closer now that he was not moving, and it kept jeering and sniggering at him and saying how *brave* it thought he was.

"No," he told himself. "It's no use worrying. I've had enough. All these years wandering and gathering things, just so some other isle can pinch them. That's it. I'm settling here. Maybe one day someone will put another 'Danger: Submerged Rocks' sign on me." And he shut his eyes and sank his toes down deep into the seafloor silt and tried to stand as still and lifeless as any other rock of the ocean.

But he could not stop his mind from working. He could not stop himself thinking.

He thought how wrong it was that the Thurlstone was allowed to roam around wrecking other people's wigs. Then he thought sadly that the *Water Mole* was the best thing he had ever, ever found. Then he thought that, actually, Oliver and Iris were the best things he had found. He began to worry about them. He began to think that maybe the jeering weed was right to hint that he'd been cowardly. Maybe Oliver had been right. Maybe he *should* go to the Hallowed Shallows and tell the other isles what that rotten-hearted Thurlstone was up to.

"Somebody's got to do *something*!" he said aloud. "And Oliver and Iris are too small, and Mr. Culpeper is just an albatross, so that somebody must be . . . er . . . *me!*"

Oooooh!

said all the seaweed, tittering in that annoying way it had. But it soon stopped, for Cliff was on the move again, striding and swimming as quickly as he could towards the same horizon that Oliver's dinghy had vanished over.

SEVEN

The sea beneath the dinghy was growing shallower. First the faces of the wading islands appeared above the waves, and then their shoulders. Oliver looked down through the clear water and saw mermaid villages clustering on the silvery sand of the seafloor. The islands set their huge stony feet down carefully, picking their way between huts and fish farms.

113

Iris peered down too, trying to spot people she knew. Merfolk were darting in shoals between the islands' feet, but Iris was too nearsighted to make out their faces.

Ahead, some of the isles had stopped, a crowd of great stony heads rising from the water. Their voices boomed across the sea, exchanging greetings and stories of their travels.

"Look!" said Oliver.

In the midst of the waiting isles stood the Thurlstone. There was no mistaking that towering outline, with the stolen submarine right on the top. The islands around it were all casting wary, envious looks at its fine wig.

Iris flapped the dinghy closer. A fire was blazing among the trees on the Thurlstone's top. Now and then a small, cavorting figure was silhouetted against the flames. The sound of drumming echoed across the water. There was no sign of those dangling glass globes.

Oliver felt awfully afraid. He remembered what Cliff had said about the Thurlstone's liking for blood. Was that why Stacey de Lacey had captured his parents? Perhaps he was hoping to impress the other Rambling Isles with human sacrifices!

"I have to go and find them!" he said.

The only answer was a snore from Iris. Tired out by all that tail-flapping, she had fallen asleep, draped over the dinghy's stern.

Oliver did not try to wake her. He could see that she was far too exhausted to help him free his parents. He pulled her into the dinghy and tucked a blanket from his rucksack over her. He looked around for Mr. Culpeper, but the albatross had flown off to talk to some of the gulls that wheeled in white clouds around the other Rambling Isles.

Oliver scrawled a note to Iris on the inside of a caramel bar wrapper, then quickly stripped down to his special swim trunks. He snapped on some goggles and a pair of frogman's flippers that he found in his rucksack, then dived into the sea. He struck out quickly towards the Thurlstone. Crowds of merpeople and shoals of silver fish darted beneath him, but they were all far too busy and excited to notice him. The Thurlstone's rocky head towered up into the darkening sky ahead of him. On its black sand beach only the surf moved, but up on its top he could hear sea monkeys cheering and squealing, pounding on stone xylophones and sealskin drums.

Oliver swam and swam. He was a good swimmer (he needed to be after all the shark- and crocodile- and piranha-infested waters that Mr. and Mrs. Crisp had made him swim in), but the Thurlstone did not seem to be getting any nearer. He realized that it was moving again, shuffling its way right to the front of that crowd of giants.

A little cold finger of panic tickled Oliver on the back of his neck. He looked back. He had already swum a long way. He was shivering slightly, and although the Hallowed Shallows might only come up to the knees of Rambling Isles, Oliver was still far out of his depth. He thought for a moment of shouting for Iris, but he wasn't sure what might happen if the Rambling Isles or the merpeople heard him and realized that a human being had come to their sacred seas.

Just then he noticed that the little cold finger tickling him wasn't panic; it was an actual finger, and it belonged to an actual sea monkey. He yelped with fright as the creature doggy-paddled around in front of him, grinning madly. "Eep!" it said, eyes blazing with reflected moonbeams. It grabbed Oliver by his wrist and started pulling him through the water, towards the Thurlstone.

For a moment Oliver struggled, fearful of capture. Then he looked again at the monkey's grinning face and changed his mind. It was trying to help him.

"Eep!" it said again, and with an answering "Eep!" another monkey appeared, sliding over a wave top and seizing Oliver by his other wrist. They chattered at each other, kicking their powerful little legs, hauling him forwards through the water. In ones and twos they seemed quite cute, he thought. Perhaps they weren't such bad creatures after all. Perhaps they just wanted to play?

A third monkey appeared. Then a fourth. The Thurlstone was definitely drawing nearer now. That rowdy party was still going on up above, but from nooks and crevices in the island's shores more monkeys were jumping down into the surf and swimming out to see what their friends had found. Their small hands stroked and prodded Oliver. They added their strength to his and he surged through the waves, closer and closer to the Thurlstone's beach. . . .

And then, all of a sudden, there were too many monkeys. They all wanted to play with Oliver, and the newcomers began to squabble with the ones who'd found him first. Some climbed onto Oliver's head. Some wrestled his right flipper off and clung gleefully to his toes as he kicked and twisted, trying to dislodge them. He started to feel as if he was swimming in wet green fur instead of water. Monkeys were using him as a raft, scrambling up onto his shoulders and crowding on his head, forcing him under. A scrabbling, squabbling ball of monkeys surrounded him as he sank, and they were so busy taunting and fighting and teasing each other that none of them stopped to wonder if the boy in their midst could breathe underwater.

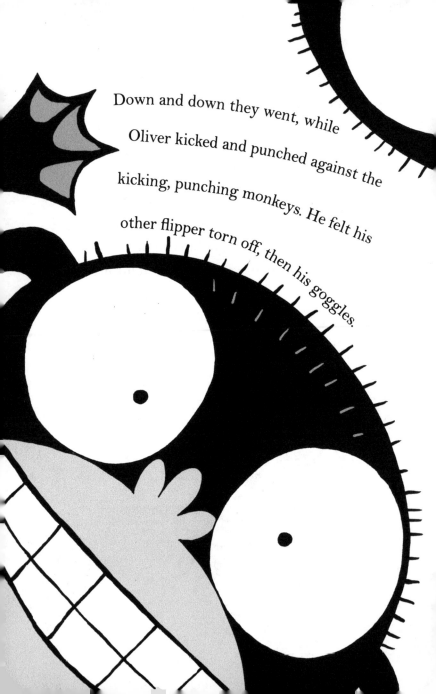

Down and down they went, while Oliver kicked and punched against the kicking, punching monkeys. He felt his other flipper torn off, then his goggles.

Strong little arms tugged him

this way and that, so that he was

afraid they'd pull him to pieces if they

didn't drown him first. At last,

with a wild jerk,

he jackknifed free of them and struck out blindly, leaving the monkeys to swirl and tumble behind him, not realizing yet that he'd broken out.

The Thurlstone's flank was a dim, dark wall in front of him. A deeper darkness showed in it. Oliver swam in, thinking it was a cleft that might hide him from the monkeys as he clawed his way back to the surface. In fact it was the opening of a narrow cave. Oliver remembered all those cracks and fissures he had noticed in the Thurlstone's sides when it first rose from the waves. Hollow, rotten to the core. That's what Cliff had said. . . .

The passage was too narrow to turn around in, so he swam on. Heart pounding, eyes bulging, sure he was about to drown, he clawed through winding, stony passages, until at last he came up gasping for air at the center of a flooded cavern.

Through a shaft in the ceiling, moonlight

slanted, shining on the rippled water. Drums and monkey chants came down too, but softly, as if from high above. Things brushed against Oliver's legs as he trod water in the middle of the cave. Weeds? Or tentacles? He thought of the squids and octopuses that had clung to the Thurlstone's eyebrows. Was this where they lived? Panicking a bit, he swam to the side of the cave and pulled himself out onto a stony ledge. Behind him the water slopped and gurgled. He imagined disappointed monsters sinking back into the depths.

An opening in the rock wall led into another passage. This one was dry, and moonlight came down it. He crept along it. It sloped steeply upwards, round, like a stone throat. Weeds and ferns grew from the walls, and he used them as handholds while he climbed.

EIGHT

Iris woke up suddenly. "Oliver?" she said, sitting up in the dinghy and looking around. Night had fallen while she slept. Moonlight and starlight silvered the sea. The dinghy rose and fell upon a gentle swell.

"He's gone," said Mr. Culpeper, swooping down to land on the side of the dinghy with a beak full of sardines. "He left you a note."

Iris looked around and saw the note that

Oliver had left, tucked into a gap between the bottom boards.

"What does it say?" she wondered.

"How would I know?" said Mr. Culpeper. "I'm an albatross."

Iris peered at the letters with her near-sighted eyes.

GONE TO THE THURLSTONE
BACK SOON
LOVE, OLIVER

"There you are then," said Mr. Culpeper.

Iris looked up. Even she could see the Thurlstone, with the *Water Mole* balanced on its top. "But what about the ARMY OF MONKEYS?" she said, flapping her fins about in agitation. "He'll be taken prisoner, just like his mom and dad!"

She launched herself over the dinghy's side and dropped with a splash into the sea. It felt good to be in the warm, scented waters of the Shallows once again, skimming over the silvery sand, flashing past the feet of Rambling Isles. But halfway to the Thurlstone she collided with a shoal of mermaids who were heading busily in the other direction.

"Ooof!" said their leader. He was a fat merman, and he was annoyed at being head-butted in the belly. "Watch where you're going, can't you?"

"Sorry," said Iris. "I'm on my way to . . ."

"To the Singing Rocks, yes, yes, come on," the merman snapped, and before she could say that, no, that wasn't where she was going at all, Iris had been swept up in the excitable shoal of young mermaids. They were all done up to the nines, with polished tails and starfish in their hair. Each carried her comb and mirror. There were a few who Iris knew; the very ones who used to laugh at her nearsightedness.

"Where are we going?" she asked as they bustled her along. She hadn't been much more than a merbaby on the last Night of the Seawigs, and she wasn't entirely sure what it involved.

"We're off to the Singing Rocks!" one of them said. "To sing our songs for the Rambling Isles. Mermaids always sing on the Night of the Seawigs, remember? Come on!"

"But I can't sing!" Iris protested, trying to turn away.

They grabbed her hand and dragged her with them. "Of course you can!" they said. "This is no time to be modest! Come *along*!"

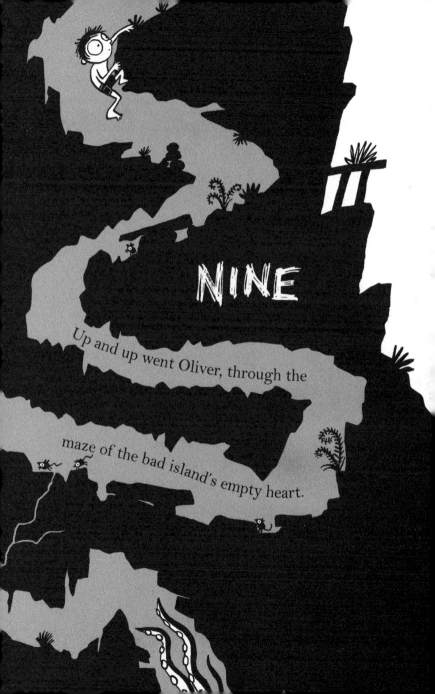

NINE

Up and up went Oliver, through the

maze of the bad island's empty heart.

It was not like climbing through a person's insides (that would have been horrid!). Everything seemed to be made of stone. The only thing that told Oliver he was inside a living being was that sometimes when he set his foot down or grabbed an out-jutting bit of passage wall, the whole lot *twitched*. The Thurlstone was ticklish, it seemed. Oliver tried to use only the weeds and ferns as handholds once he'd worked that out. Not all of them had deep roots. Twice he nearly fell, while leaves and clumps of rooty earth went tumbling down the shaft to spatter into the black pool where the squids and octopuses were waiting, tentacles crossed, hoping that he'd fall. But Oliver was a good climber (all the mountains and crags and lost temples he'd climbed with his mom and dad had made sure of that) and before long he was at the top.

He crawled out of a crack in the summit of the Thurlstone. The *Water Mole* and the other shipwrecks loomed over him. Monkey drums boomed, and stone xylophones clattered. The monkeys were having a wild old time, dancing around their fire, toasting sea anemones on sticks, and painting glasses and mustaches on the old stone heads. None of them noticed Oliver as he crept like a damp ghost between the trees.

Soon he reached the temple. Outside its great stone entrance was a pool, and on the pool the two glass globes that held his parents floated. Mr. and Mrs. Crisp were asleep, huddled in the bottoms of the globes, which clinked gently against each other from time to time, like wineglasses.

"Mom!" called Oliver softly. "Dad!"

They did not stir. Poor things, they were just as exhausted as Iris after all their adventures.

"Mom!" he shouted, wading into the pool and banging his fists against the globes.

Still his parents did not wake, although Dad rolled over and muttered something in his dreams. But someone had heard Oliver. A voice from behind him said, "Ha!"

He turned around.

There stood Stacey de Lacey, with his army of monkeys around him. Some of them were still beating their drums and banging their xylophones. One held a tray of biscuits, another a cool drink for Stacey, and two others fanned him with big peacock-feather fans. The rest were just bibbling about like mad windup toys, full of excitement at all the mischief that lay ahead.

"You!" said Stacey de Lacey, pointing rudely at Oliver. "So here you are, come to thieve and sneak and spoil my plans!"

"I just want my mom and dad back!" Oliver promised.

"Well, you can't have them!" jeered Stacey. "The Thurlstone needs them. They are the finishing touches on his wig. They could make all the difference. They're just the sort of thing that will make him stand out."

"But why do you care so much about the Thurlstone winning?" Oliver asked miserably.

"Ah!" said Stacey de Lacey. "We've got a deal, me and the Thurlstone. If I help him win this seawig thing, then he'll help me. Imagine the power I'll have, with this great big giant at my command! And other Rambling Isles will follow the Thurlstone when they see his wonderful wig! The winner of Seawigs Night is a sort of king; they'll have to do as he says. We'll stomp New York, smash London, sit on Shanghai. The whole world will tremble before us! Nobody will *dare* say I've got a girly name then!"

"But you *have* got a girly name," grumbled Oliver.

"MONKEYS!" howled Stacey de Lacey.

Oliver tried to fend the monkeys off, but soon he was pinned down under a gibbering heap of them. Meanwhile, some others had gone rushing into a side chamber of the temple and reappeared bowling a third glass globe. Some held it steady while the rest unscrewed its lid. Then Oliver was monkey handled into it, and the lid screwed shut behind him.

Stacey de Lacey grinned in at him, his leering face stretched out of shape by the thick glass. "Now the Thurlstone's wig is finished!" he chortled. "Not just *two* stupid Crisps, but the whole set!"

Tittering with mischief, the monkeys rolled Oliver away. Mr. and Mrs. Crisp had been woken by the noise and were sitting up inside their globes, watching sadly as their son was trundled past them.

"I'm sorry!" mouthed Oliver.

A reef of dark rocks rose from the Hallowed Shallows, with the waves breaking whitely around it. Wet stone shone in the moonlight. The mermaids scrambled through the surf and up onto the reef's rocky ledges. There they sat, each with her comb and her mirror and her long hair blown sideways on the breeze. Their plump choirmaster bobbed like a seal in the waves and clapped his hands to get the mermaids' attention. "Just time for a quick practice, girls! Sing up!"

So they sang, and their voices blended with the voices of the sea and wind. All over the Hallowed Shallows the Rambling Isles forgot their nervousness and listened. Up on the Thurlstone's head Oliver and his mom and dad heard that song, and it sent shivers down their spines. (They couldn't listen for long, though. They were busy being rolled across the Thurlstone's summit by those monkeys and dangled over its edge.)

"Stop, stop, stop!" the fat merman shouted, clapping his hands over his ears. The song of mermaids was meant to sound strange and unearthly, but not *this* strange and unearthly.

"Someone's singing flat!" he said accusingly, glaring at the rows of singers.

Iris knew it was her. She blushed deep red. The merman spotted her and pointed. "You! Sing for me!"

Iris drew a deep breath and sang as loudly and sweetly as

she could. An awful, strangled note emerged, so piercing that the nearest mermaids' mirrors cracked.

"Stop! Stop!" the merman shouted. "What a disgraceful racket! What were you thinking of, joining our choir with a voice like that! Be off with you!"

Iris started to explain that she hadn't meant to join the choir at all, then decided that there wasn't time and splashed back into the sea. She couldn't imagine why she'd wanted to find her way home to all these silly merpeople. Her new friends were much more fun. All she cared about now was rescuing Oliver.

TEN

The Hallowed Shallows were crowded with Rambling Isles now, hundreds of them, some large, some small. They seemed to be waiting for something. Oliver waited too, dangling from the Thurlstone's brow, his glass globe swinging to and fro in its creaking basket of ropes. When would the judging begin?

Stacey de Lacey was running about busily on the Thurlstone's head, shouting orders at his monkeys while they did a bit of last-minute polishing and tidied scraps of seawig that had been blown skew-whiff by the wind.

At last, on the far horizon, a tiny speck appeared, drawing quickly closer. The islands all mumbled and muttered to each other, turning to look. Soon Oliver could see that the approaching thing was another Rambling Isle, striding purposefully through the waves. On either side of it the wave crests foamed, and the foam took on the form of galloping horses. It was the Chief Island, who had won the last Night of the

Seawigs. The white horses of the sea formed an honor guard for her, and the mermaids on the Singing Rocks started to sing again, properly now that they didn't have Iris helping. The Chief Island (her name was Dambulay) waded into the Shallows and stopped. On her summit towered a massive wig of trees and flowers and grasses, with rainbows knotted in it, and the prows of Viking longships jutting out like ornate hairpins. She looked at her fellow islands with pride and sadness, and then quickly shook her head, so that the old wig came apart, the rainbows drifting away, the rotten timbers of the ships tumbling down her sides into the sea.

"Ahhh!" said the Rambling Isles, and "Oooh!" Even the Thurlstone made a deep rumbling sound, out of respect for Dambulay's wonderful wig.

"Never mind," said Dambulay sadly. "It was a good wig, but it was old, and now I can start again and collect a whole new one. But first we must see who here has the finest seawig. Which of us has found the prettiest things on our wanderings? Who shall be the winner tonight, and Chief Island for the next seven years?"

The islands shifted a little. The ones whose wigs were really poor or had suffered in the wind slunk backwards into deeper water. Some eyed up the drifting bits of Dambulay's wig that still bobbed upon the waves, wondering if they could make some last-minute changes without the others noticing. The prouder ones preened themselves, hoping to attract the votes of their neighbors. The island with the wig of drizzled sand drew many admiring looks. So did another, which had a crown of whalebones. But none could compare to the splendor of the Thurlstone, with its shipwrecks and those three glass globes, from which three captive humans gawked. One by one the islands turned until they were all gazing at it.

Oliver, trapped in his hanging globe, pounded his hands against the inside of the glass and shouted, "No! It's not fair! The Thurlstone cheated!" But the mermaids were singing still, and their voices drowned out his protests. His parents waved and shouted too, but the Rambling Isles thought they were only pleading for their freedom. Captive humans! How original! No island had worn captive humans for *centuries*!

"Thurlstone!" said one of the isles in a deep, rumbly voice.

"Thurlstone!" said another, softer.

"Thurlstone!" cried a third in a voice like the boom of surf in deserted coves.

Iris popped up beside the Thurlstone's left knee, red-faced and breathless after her hasty swim from the reef. She pointed up at the isle and shouted, but there was no way she could make herself heard over the voices of the Rambling Isles.

"Thurlstone! Thurlstone! Thurlstone!" Even the one with the wig of whalebones, who had been hoping to win, saw which way the tide was turning and added his voice to those of the others: "Thurlstone! Let Thurlstone be the winner."

Just then the song of the mermaids rose in a wild crescendo, and suddenly Iris saw how she might be able to save Oliver and his family, even if all else was lost. She took a deep breath and sang the same note she had sung for the merman choirmaster a few moments before. She sang louder this time, as loud and as shrill as she could. She sang until her face turned purple. Before, her voice had been enough to break the mermaids' mirrors. This time it made the Rambling Isles clap their

hands over their ears, and put the other mermaids off their song.

Oliver, swinging in his globe, saw a fine frost of cracks start to spread across the glass. *Tisssh! Crasssh! Smasssh!* The three globes shattered. Icefalls of glass cascaded down the Thurlstone's cliffs. Into the sea dropped Mr. and Mrs. Crisp.

But what of Oliver? Iris peered about, trying not to be distracted by the hoots of the angry islands, who were all outraged that a mere mermaid had dared to interrupt that solemn moment.

Ah, there he was! Clinging to a root that jutted from the Thurlstone's rocky forehead. But just as Iris saw him, a great smother of foam came down on her. The Thurlstone turned towards her, swirling the skirts of the sea.

Iris quickly darted out of the way as the Thurlstone's huge foot tried to squash her.

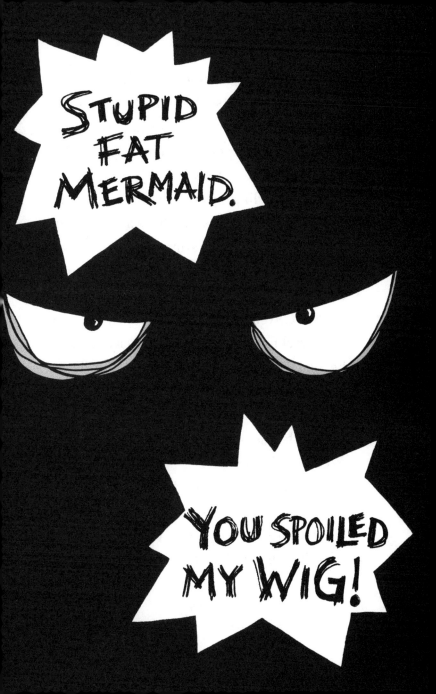

She plunged down under it, almost to the silver sand of the seafloor, and then rose up on the other side. As she broke the surface there, Mr. Culpeper came flapping over her, squawking, "Here they are!" She saw Mr. and Mrs. Crisp, clinging together, tossed up and down like two corks on the waves that the angry island was creating. She seized each of them by a hand and swam with them to calmer water.

But Oliver knew nothing about any of this.

Clutching at roots and rocky pimples, he had heaved himself back up the Thurlstone's steep face. There he saw sea monkeys running in every direction, while furious Stacey de Lacey kicked them about like furry green footballs.

"It's all gone wrong!" Stacey raged. "We'll be disqualified! Unless . . ."

"Gaaargh!" roared the Thurlstone. Other islands blundered away from it, scared of its

156

rage and the way it lashed its clumsy stone fists about like massive hammers. Stacey de Lacey scrambled onto his viewing platform on the island's brow and grabbed his megaphone. "The Thurlstone is still the winner!" he bellowed. "You chose him, and he won, fair and square! And now you'd better do what he says, or my monkeys will come and mess your wigs up!"

Sea monkeys spilled down the Thurlstone's face like a river of snot. They spread across the ocean, gibbering with wild glee as the waves lifted them up and down. But above the shouting of Stacey de Lacey and the roars of the Thurlstone, the hoots of frightened isles and the squeals of the monkeys, a new voice boomed out.

"STOP!" it said.

The Rambling Isles looked around. The monkeys too. Even the Thurlstone stopped roaring and glanced over its huge stone shoulder.

157

Another Rambling Isle had arrived. A small and shabby isle, with nothing on its head but the sad remnants of a not-very-good wig, and a confused narwhal that it had just scooped up. At the sight of him, Iris jumped clean out of the water and turned a cartwheel above the Crisps' bewildered heads.

Oliver, looking down from the Thurlstone's brow, grinned a great grin and whispered, "Cliff!"

Cliff stood up as tall as he could, and the narwhal fell off his head. He shook a fist at the Thurlstone and shouted something about stolen ships and kidnappings, but the surf was bursting against him, and all that most of his listeners heard was "Blarrgle!"

Oliver, from his high vantage point, could see that the poor island's knees were knocking together, but still Cliff stood his ground as the Thurlstone, with seabed-shaking stomps, strode angrily towards him.

Poor Cliff! All the way from the Sarcastic Sea he had kept telling himself that his fellow Rambling Isles would help him to teach the Thurlstone a lesson. Now he could see that they were all as scared of it as he was. As they edged nervously away, he realized that he was going to have to face it alone.

Which was very bad, because the Thurlstone was bigger and stronger and fiercer than Cliff, and up on its head Stacey de Lacey was yelling, "Smash him, Thurlstone! Bash him up! Stamp him down!"

"Leave him alone!" shouted Oliver, jumping up from his hiding place. A monkey drum rolled past him as the Thurlstone lurched towards Cliff, and Oliver snatched it and flung it at Stacey de Lacey. It missed, but it made Stacey look around, and he forgot about Cliff and charged angrily at Oliver instead.

Oliver ran away from him, zigzagging between the trees, looking for something he could use to defend himself. Near the pool by the temple he found one of the peacock-feather fans lying where a careless monkey had dropped it. It looked a flimsy, feather-dustery sort of thing, but he picked it up anyway.

That was when the idea came to him.

He could hear Stacey de Lacey panting through the trees behind him, spluttering threats and curses. The ground beneath him shivered as the Thurlstone let out another cry of rage. Oliver ran between the trees to where one of those fissures opened, the cracks that led down into the island's hollow insides. He took a deep breath and jumped in. *Dump—bump—crash*, he went, bruising himself as he tumbled down through stony tubes and crannies.

He snatched at out-juttings of rock to slow himself, and the Thurlstone flinched just as it had before. How could something so big and stony-seeming be so ticklish? Oliver wondered. And what would happen when he really started tickling?

He found a foothold, raised his feather fan, and set to work.

* * *

The Thurlstone swung a huge fist at Cliff. Cliff ducked, and the blow missed by a whisker. The Thurlstone growled and rumbled, readying itself to strike again.

But suddenly it stopped. Something was *moving* inside it. Something that *tickled.* . . . It writhed. A shipwreck dropped off its wig and splashed into the sea. *"Arrrararaggaharauaaraga!"* said the Thurlstone (or something along those lines). Another ship fell—the *Water Mole* this time. It landed near the spot where Mr. and Mrs. Crisp were treading water, and Iris hustled them aboard it.

"Stoppit!" howled the Thurlstone, but Oliver wouldn't stop. Deep in the bad old isle's insides, he tickled and he tickled, mercilessly jabbing his feather fan into all the cracks and fissures he could reach, wriggling and jiggling it there.

The Thurlstone clutched its sides and howled. It stumbled and staggered, throwing up sheets of spray, making waves that slapped against the faces of the other Rambling Isles and rocked the *Water Mole* and her passengers wildly up and down. A stone head tumbled off the Thurlstone's summit. A few last sea monkeys jumped off the cliffs like rats abandoning a sinking ship, cannonballing into the water. The ancient temple quivered, cracked, crumbled. Bits and pieces of it cascaded past the Thurlstone's face to smash into the water. Other bits of his wig came loose too, wreaths of seaweed, boulders, trees. . . .

"You vandal!" Stacey de Lacey screamed, dodging a toppling stone head and shouting down the crack that Oliver had vanished into. "You spoilsport! You're ruining everything!"

Down beneath his feet, Oliver just went on tickling and tickling. . . .

Until, with a creak, a black crack opened, splitting the Thurlstone's summit in two.

Other, smaller cracks spread out from it. Stacey de Lacey watched in horror as they surrounded him. More creaks and groans and straining sounds filled the air. The Thurlstone had quaked and quivered and shuddered and shaken so much that it was coming completely to pieces. Down on the water, Iris and the Crisps watched cracks cover the Thurlstone's stupid, startled face like a black net. Then, in a slither of shards and a cloud of dust and upflung spray, the Rambling Isle exploded.

For a moment they saw Stacey de Lacey clinging to the top of one great fragment, yelling as it toppled. For a moment they thought they saw Oliver, tumbling free with a big feather fan flapping like a wing above him. Then the spray hid everything.

Oliver hit the water hard as the Thurlstone came apart around him. He plunged deep enough to brush his fingers over the silver sand beneath, and came up gasping for air. He trod water and looked around, while the upflung spray fell upon the waves like rain.

There was no Thurlstone anymore, only a few scattered chunks, small islets whose heads barely poked above the water even here in the Shallows. One by one they opened little black beady eyes of their own and blinked. They were brand-new Rambling Isles, bashful in the presence of so many bigger ones.

Oliver laughed, swimming between them until ahead of him he saw the *Water Mole*, still just about afloat, with his mom and dad and Iris and Mr. Culpeper all waving at him from its upper deck.

Iris pulled him aboard, and he ran and

hugged Mom, then Dad. The ancient submarine was sinking fast, but Cliff waded over and supported it before it could settle to the seafloor.

"Wow! That was really amazing!" said a strand of Sarcastic Seaweed, hanging down in front of Cliff's face, and it sounded as if it really meant it.

The other islands shuffled closer, trying to look as if they had been right at Cliff's side all along and not a bit scared of the Thurlstone. Some mumbled that Cliff had done well; others explained that they had never trusted the Thurlstone. A few of the quicker-thinking ones scooped up bits of the Thurlstone's scattered wig and added them to their own, because it was pretty clear that a new winner would have to be chosen.

It was Dambulay who was the first to say "Thank you." She looked at Iris and Oliver, then at Cliff. "Thank you. You have saved us from awarding the greatest honor of our kind to a bad creature who did not deserve it. You have been brave, while we were cowardly. What is your name?"

"Cliff," said Cliff, blushing a bit. "This is my seawig," he added, scooping up the *Water Mole* and setting it on his top again. "The Thurlstone stole it from me. There were some other bits too, but they got lost."

The Rambling Isles all looked at him. The *Water Mole* did not look nearly as splendid on top of Cliff as it had when the Thurlstone wore it. The strands of weed that he had carried with him from the Sarcastic Sea did their best to look decorative, and Mr. Culpeper perched on the *Water Mole*'s bow with his wings outspread, but it still looked a bit shabby and scruffy. Even so, Dambulay turned to the other islands and said, "I think it is clear what we must do. Cliff is the bravest of us, and his seawig is certainly the most . . . interesting. He is the winner of this Night of the Seawigs."

"Yay!" shouted Iris and Oliver and Mr. Culpeper. Mr. and Mrs. Crisp clapped politely—they were a bit confused, but they were starting to get the hang of things. Even the weed looked pleased.

But Cliff slowly shook his head.

"Not me," he said. "I can't hang around here in the Shallows, being feted and fussed over. I don't care about this Seawig competition anymore. Let Thrumcap be the winner, or Dimsey. I have to take my friends home."

Then, with all the other Rambling Isles looking on, he turned and waded away. Up on his head Mr. and Mrs. Crisp fetched out their cameras and took photo after photo of the watching isles and the mermaids. But either because of some magic of the Shallows or

because the cameras had been battered too badly during their adventures, not one of those pictures ever came out.

As for Oliver, he just clung to the *Water Mole*'s barnacled rail and stared, trying to take it all in. He saw the unearthly purplish sky and the pale sea, the white horses galloping in the wave crests, the mermaids playing in Cliff's wake like dolphins. He saw the Rambling Isles in all their finery. He did his best to fix it in his mind forever, and unlike the photographs, his memories *did* come out. He kept them always, and they never faded.

Not far away, a fragment of the roof from the Thurlstone's temple floated on the waves.

Stacey de Lacey sat on it, bedraggled and alone, using another, smaller piece of flotsam for a paddle. He was paddling himself away from the Hallowed Shallows as quickly as he could. He was hoping that, if the sea stayed calm and the wind in the right direction, he might paddle all the way home. He wondered if his parents had noticed that he'd been away.

"Eep?" said a little voice. Webbed paws appeared over the edge of his raft. A sea monkey pulled itself aboard and snuggled down against Stacey's left knee. He patted its head, feeling rather glad that he still had a friend left.

"Eep!" said another monkey, scrambling out of the sea behind him.

"Eep! Eep! Eeber! Eeeple!" said a dozen more.

"No!" cried Stacey. "Back in the sea with you! There isn't room!"

But there's no arguing with sea monkeys, and the sea

around his raft was green with them. They swarmed aboard. When there wasn't a single inch of bare wood left without a little wet green body sitting

on it, they started sitting on
Stacey de Lacey instead, and
when there wasn't a single inch of
him without a monkey, they took
to sitting on top of each other,
until a teetering, bickering mound
of monkeys was piled high on the wal-
lowing raft, with Stacey de Lacey in the
middle of it somewhere, still glumly
paddling.

ELEVEN

Mr. and Mrs. Crisp were very meek during the journey home. They knew that their terrible adventures had all happened because they'd been so eager to explore the islands, and they knew of the dangers that Oliver had braved to rescue them. "No more exploring for us," they agreed, sitting with Oliver, Iris, and Mr. Culpeper beside the campfire they had lit on Cliff's head.

But Oliver knew they didn't mean it. After all the thrilling new things they'd seen, they would soon be itching to go exploring again. They wouldn't even have to worry about money anymore, because the old trunks that they'd dragged out of the *Water Mole* to use as seats around the fire turned out to be stuffed full of Spanish gold. For the moment, though, they seemed very happy to be safe and back with Oliver again. And they were happier still a few days later, when Cliff waded into Deepwater Bay, and they saw their house and the dear old explorermobile standing where they had left them.

Oliver wasn't happy, though. He was glad to see dry land again, but he didn't feel that surge of joy he'd felt when Dad drove them down the lane to the house that first day. He still wanted a home just as badly, but he wanted something else now too: he wanted to be with Cliff and Iris. He was going to miss them. He would even miss crotchety Mr. Culpeper.

So he stood quietly watching while the shore came closer, and his mom and dad did a happy-to-be-home dance on Cliff's golden sand. And when they said, "Look, Ollie, it's our house!" and "Aren't you glad to be back?" he nodded and said that he was. But Mr. and Mrs. Crisp could tell he wasn't, and they looked solemnly at one another. They both knew how sweet and sad it could be to want two different things so completely.

"Don't worry," said Mr. Crisp, putting an arm around Oliver's shoulders. "We'll find a way."

Mrs. Crisp knelt down and tapped politely on Cliff's forehead. "We were wondering," she said, "if you've nowhere else to go, perhaps you'd like to stay here in Deepwater Bay? It looks so much nicer with an island in it."

So Cliff found a comfortable spot for

himself just offshore, and that night the Crisp family slept in actual beds, inside a proper house, for the first time in years. (Iris made up a bed for herself in the bath.) Early the next morning Oliver took the dinghy up the coast to Farsight Cove with Iris swimming alongside.

The beach optician was in his usual spot on the sand, and he looked very startled when Iris came out of the sea. He had never really believed in mermaids either, and his beach optician's stall was just an excuse to get away from his noisy family and spend a few hours each day sitting quietly by the sea. But he hid his surprise as best he could, and tested Iris's eyes, and presented her with a very fetching pair of spectacles.

"Wow!" she said, gazing about her at the cliffs, the sand, the sea. Suddenly everything looked very sharp and clear. She wasn't sure she liked it, though she supposed she would get used to it in time. "So *that's* what you look like!" she said, peering at Oliver through the thick lenses. "Oh."

"What do you mean, 'Oh'?" asked Oliver.

"Nothing," said Iris.

* * *

Meanwhile, Mr. Crisp had been drawing plans on the backs of old envelopes, and Mrs. Crisp had been telephoning local builders and asking if they would accept payment in ancient Spanish doubloons. It turned out that they would, and soon the Crisps' old house had been dismantled and rebuilt on top of Cliff. ("It's the best wig a Rambling Isle ever had!" he said delightedly when it was finished.)

Of course that meant that there was no longer room for the *Water Mole*, but the old submarine wasn't really suited to being out in the open air anyway, and its timbers were beginning to crumble as they dried out. So they carefully lowered it to the bottom of Deepwater Bay, and Iris set up house inside it. When Oliver came home from school in the afternoons, he'd often dive down to visit her, holding his breath for as long as he could to see her latest improvements.

Now that she could see clearly, Iris had

grown rather house-proud, and she had gathered odds and ends from the seabed to decorate her new home. Oliver thought the old toilet bowl she had on display in the center of her kitchen table looked rather odd, but she'd arranged such a colorful collection of live sea anemones in it that he had to confess it brightened up the place. She'd also hung up several mirrors, which Oliver noticed were all cracked, but he was too polite to ask if she'd been singing. The more she showed him, the faster he'd nod and approve it all, as his cheeks went redder and redder from lack of air. But Iris was always pleased to see him making the effort.

* * *

Even Mr. Culpeper stayed. He complained that the island was getting very built up, and he enjoyed telling other visiting birds that *he* could remember when it was all just rocks and grass. But he built himself a large, raggedy nest on the roof just above Oliver's bedroom and enjoyed waking Oliver up each morning by leaning down and shouting "Time for school!" through the window. Oliver didn't mind, though: he *enjoyed* school.

Mr. and Mrs. Crisp made a little bridge to link Cliff to the mainland, wide enough for the explorermobile or the cars of visiting friends to drive across. But it wasn't a permanent bridge: it could be folded back onto Cliff's shores whenever the Crisps wanted to remember that they really did live on an island. And sometimes, on Oliver's school holidays or on other days when they just felt like it, they'd say to Cliff, "This feels like an exploring day." Then they would fold the bridge away, and Cliff would wade off in search of strange seas and forgotten coves, with Mr. and Mrs. Crisp safe and snug in their own living room, Mr. Culpeper keeping watch from his nest, and Iris and Oliver riding on the beach.

It was by far the most comfortable way to go exploring.

DRAWING YOUR OWN SEA MONKEY
IS EEP! EEP! SO EASY!
LET'S GET STARTED...

DID YOU LIKE THIS NOT-SO-IMPOSSIBLE TALE?

THEN TURN THE PAGE AND TRAVEL TO **SPACE!**
GET READY FOR A SNEAK PEEK OF

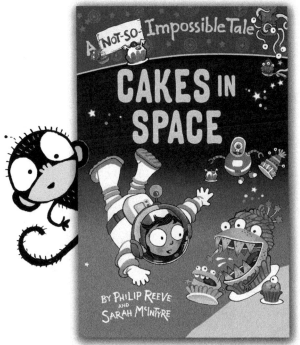

A NOT-SO- Impossible Tale

CAKES IN SPACE

BY PHILIP REEVE AND SARAH MCINTYRE

AVAILABLE NOW!

The trouble with space is,
there's so much of it.

An ocean of blackness
without any shore.

A never-ending nothing.

And here, all alone in the million billion miles of midnight, is one solitary moving speck. A fragile parcel filled with sleeping people and their dreams.

A ship.

To travel from the Earth to the moon takes a few days. From Earth to Mars, a few months. To Jupiter, a few years, and to Neptune and Pluto a few years more. But Astra was traveling farther still. Much, much farther. The world called Nova Mundi, where Astra and her family were going to live, was so far from Earth that it would take them 199 years to get there.

A HUNDRED AND NINETY-NINE YEARS ??!

yelled Astra when her mother first told her. "We can't sit in a spaceship for one hundred and ninety-nine years! It'll be so *boring*! There won't even be anything to look at out of the window, even if spaceships *have* windows . . . which they probably don't! And I'll be *old* by the time we arrive! I'll be . . ." She counted on her fingers. "I'll be two hundred and nine years old! I'll be all wrinkly!"

But Astra's mother just laughed, bouncing Astra's baby brother, Alf, up and down on her knee until he laughed, too. "Don't worry, Astra. We won't be awake. When we go aboard the spaceship, we'll get into special sleeping pods. . . ."

"Like beds?" asked Astra.

"A little like beds," agreed her father. "And a little like freezers."

"Won't we be cold?" asked Astra with a shiver. She imagined herself snuggling down among the frozen peas and Popsicles, an ice cream cake for a pillow.

"We won't *feel* cold," said her mother. "We won't feel anything. We'll be fast asleep. The machines that run the ship will cool us right down so that we don't age. Then the ship will steer itself to Nova Mundi while we sleep, and when we get there it will wake us, and we'll feel as if only a single night has passed. And we'll be at our new home!"

"A whole new world!" said Dad.

"Nova Mundi!" said Astra.

She was excited to be going to Nova Mundi. She had seen videos and pictures of it. She and Mom and Dad and Alf were going to live in a big house there, between the wide green ocean and the fern forests, with a garden of blue grass. They would work at making the new planet ready for other people from Earth.

But she still didn't like the sound of this long, cold journey, even if she was going to be asleep.

"Will there be dreams?" she asked.

"Only nice ones," her mom promised.

And that's how it was. They took a shuttle from the spaceport.

Everybody's hair started to misbehave.

"I feel sick!" complained a girl in a nearby seat, and her mother quickly passed her a bag. Astra's dad looked a little bit green, too.

"It feels like falling," he said, taking a space-sickness pill.

But Astra didn't mind the feeling. She liked it! Falling felt good, as long as she didn't have to worry about hitting the ground. She liked the thought that they were going to fall all the way to Nova Mundi.